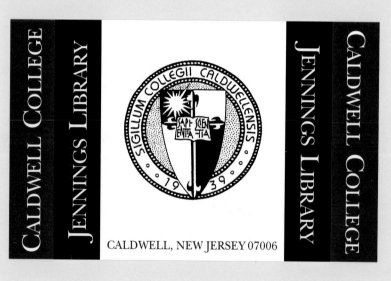

Preschool to the Rescue

BY Judy Sierra

ILLUSTRATED BY Will Hillenbrand

GULLIVER BOOKS

HARCOURT, INC.

SAN DIEGO   NEW YORK   LONDON

Text copyright © 2001 by Judy Sierra
Illustrations copyright © 2001 by Will Hillenbrand

Library of Congress Cataloging-in-Publication Data
Sierra, Judy.
Preschool to the rescue/by Judy Sierra; illustrated by Will Hillenbrand.—1st. ed.
p. cm.
"Gulliver Books."
Summary: When a mud puddle traps a pizza van, police car, tow truck, and other vehicles, a group of preschoolers comes along and saves the day.
[1. Mud—Fiction. 2. Helpfulness—Fiction. 3. Stories in rhyme.] I. Hillenbrand, Will, ill. II. Title.
PZ8.3.S577Pr 2001
[E]—dc21   99-6475
ISBN 0-15-202035-7

First edition
H G F E D C B A
Printed in Hong Kong

The illustrations in this book were created in mixed media on vellum, painted on both sides.
The display type was set in Basketcase.
The text type was set in Clearface Gothic Bold.
Printed by South China Printing Company, Ltd., Hong Kong
This book was printed on totally chlorine-free Nymolla Matte Art paper.
Production supervision by Sandra Grebenar and Ginger Boyer
Designed by Kaelin Chappell and Will Hillenbrand
Jacket design by Cathy Riggs and Barry Age

For Ian
— J. S. and W. H.

Once there was a mud puddle, and it was sleepy,
it was creepy, it was deeper-than-you'd-think.
When something went into that mud puddle,
the mud puddle didn't want to let go.

One afternoon, the pizza man was driving along in his pizza van.
Beep-beep! "This mud puddle can't be very deep," said the pizza man.
He drove his pizza van into the sleepy, creepy puddle.

Police car to the rescue!

"Don't scream, don't shout. I'll push you out," said the policewoman.

Glurp.

The pizza van was stuck in the mud.
The police car was stuck in the mud.
Stuck in the gluey, gooey mud.

Tow truck to the rescue!

"It's a cinch. I'll winch you out,"
said the tow-truck driver.

Blurp.

The pizza van was stuck in the mud.
The police car was stuck in the mud.
The tow truck was stuck in the mud.
Stuck—*yuck!*—in the muckity mud.

Backhoe to the rescue!

"I'll use my rig to dig you out,"
said the backhoe driver.

Flurp.

The pizza van was stuck in the mud.
The police car was stuck in the mud.
The tow truck was stuck in the mud.
The backhoe was stuck in the mud.
Trapped tight in the mighty mud.

Fire engine to the rescue!

"Quick! Get the hose," said the fire captain.
"We'll spray this icky mud away."

Plurp!

The pizza van was stuck in the mud.
The police car was stuck in the mud.
The tow truck was stuck in the mud.
The backhoe was stuck in the mud.
The fire engine was stuck in the mud.
All of them caught in the naughty mud.

Preschool to the rescue!

"No reason to fuss. Mud can't stop us!" said the children.

And they went to work with shovels and sand, and rocks and bricks, and rubber bands and Popsicle sticks.

"Get ready . . . Get set . . . GO!"

The fire engine roared out of the mud.

The backhoe chugged out of the mud.

The tow truck rolled out of the mud.

The police car screeched out of the mud.

The pizza van bounced out of the mud.

Everyone shouted, "Hooray! Hooray!"
for the girls and boys who saved the day.

But the preschoolers hadn't finished yet.

They mixed mud pies and mud cakes and
mud muffins and mud cookies and mud pizzas.

And that was the end of the sleepy, creepy, deeper-than-you'd-think mud puddle.